DREAMWORKS

SHE-RA
AND THE
PRINCESSES OF POWER

REBEL PRINCESS GUIDE

BY TRACEY WEST

SCHOLASTIC INC.

TABLE OF CONTENTS

~~How to Be a Princess~~

~~Strategic Manual for Princess Skills, Weaponry, and Tactics~~

~~Important Princess Stuff~~

REBEL PRINCESS GUIDE

Everything I thought I knew about princesses is wrong.

It all happened so fast. One day, I was a Horde soldier, trained to fight princesses. The next day, a magic sword transformed me into She-Ra, Princess of Power.

Right now, I have no idea how to be a princess or control my powers. But one thing I learned in the Horde is how to study. I am going to pay attention, take notes, and train from sunup until sundown. I am going to slay this princess thing!

-Adora

REPORT: MY STORY SO FAR

- How I went from being a Horde soldier to a princess, the sworn enemy of every Horde soldier

- My background in the Horde, who took me in when I was a baby. My earliest memories are of training with the other cadets in the Fright Zone

- How everything changed when I discovered the Sword of Protection

LIFE IN THE FRIGHT ZONE

AS I'M STARTING TO FIGURE OUT, the Fright Zone isn't exactly the best place to grow up. As Bow says, "There's a reason they call it the Fright Zone and not the Fun Zone."

The Fright Zone is pretty bleak. There are no flowers and no cute animals—just metal buildings and machines spewing out gray smoke all day and all night. Nobody ever complained, because we didn't know there was anything better out there on Etheria. Also, we were too afraid of Hordak, the commander of the Horde. And we knew that complainers got banished to Beast Island.

HORDAK

Every day, we trained to be soldiers. This included:

- Study   **PHEW!**
- Exercise
- Endless battle simulations
- Sleep

THERE WASN'T MUCH ELSE TO DO!

I guess I was luckier than most Horde recruits, though. Shadow Weaver, Hordak's second in command, took me under her wing. That made me feel special.

SHADOW WEAVER

CATRA

CATRA AND ME WHEN WE WERE KIDS

But the best thing about the Fright Zone was Catra. She and I did everything together. We made up games to play. We told each other stories. And we stuck up for each other when other cadets got mean. I wouldn't have survived in the Fright Zone without her.

THEN
EVERYTHING CHANGED

PART OF ME REALLY LIKED ALL THE TRAINING. I worked hard at it, and I was about to be promoted to force captain. But then Catra and I took an unauthorized trip into the Whispering Woods, and that's when everything changed . . .

- I crashed the skiff we were riding and passed out.

- I woke up in a clearing and saw a beautiful, glowing sword!

- When I touched it, weird visions flooded into my head.

- I heard a voice saying, "Balance must be restored. Etheria must seek a hero."

- I discovered that I could read the language of the First Ones, the early inhabitants of Etheria.

- When I spoke the words, "For the honor of Grayskull!" I transformed into an incredibly powerful princess named She-Ra! ♡

THAT'S ME!

My life as a Horde soldier was over. Now I was a princess: the sworn enemy of the Horde.

It's a good thing I met Glimmer and Bow when I did, or I never would have learned the truth about the princesses of Etheria.

BRIGHT MOON CASTLE

CRYSTAL CASTLE

GLIMMER

SO, THIS IS WHAT HAPPENS WHEN I TRANSFORM

IT'S HARD TO DESCRIBE WHAT IT FEELS LIKE when I transform into She-Ra. It's kind of like, "Whoa!" and then "What?" and then everything gets super bright. And then the light fades, and I feel bigger, stronger, and taller.

When I'm She-Ra, I feel like I can do anything. Like I'm unstoppable. My new outfit is pretty cool, too.

When I'm Adora, I pull back my hair to keep it out of my face while I'm in action. But when I'm She-Ra, having a mane of long, flowing hair just feels so right.

ME FINDING THE
SWORD

The Sword of
Protection is what
lets me transform
into She-Ra.

Are these the
coolest boots, or
what? Not only do they
look awesome, but they're
really comfortable. I've tested
them on ice, snow, and mud, and
I can run faster, jump higher, and kick
harder with them on.

SO COOL!

THE SWORD OF PROTECTION

MY SWORD IS REALLY POWERFUL—which is why I don't understand why it didn't come with any instructions. I really can't wait to uncover all of its secrets.

STUFF I KNOW ABOUT MY SWORD

- It was made by the First Ones.

- I found it in the Whispering Woods.

- Nobody can use it to turn into She-Ra except for me. (At least, nobody I've met yet.)

- The runestone in the hilt is keyed to She-Ra, Princess of Power. You can see it sparkling in the hilt, but the blade of the sword is actually part of the runestone, too.

STUFF I DON'T KNOW ABOUT MY SWORD

- I know that my sword can change shapes, but I don't know how to control it yet! And why does it turn into useless stuff, like a mug, a jug, and a weird musical instrument?

- Light Hope says that one of the functions of the runestone is to "heal and restore balance." But no matter how hard I try, I can't figure out how to use the sword to heal anything!

REPORT: THE BEST FRIEND SQUAD

I MET GLIMMER AND BOW in the Whispering Woods after I found the sword. We didn't start out as friends. They captured me because I was a Horde soldier and brought me to Bright Moon. But along the way, they figured out that I was really a princess, and I learned that princesses aren't evil.

It really messed with my head when I found out that everything I'd learned in the Horde had been a lie. But Glimmer and Bow helped me through it, and they didn't judge me. So pretty soon we became the Best Friend Squad, along with my horse, Swift Wind.

I know it sounds corny, but together, the Best Friend Squad can do anything! (Wow, that sounds even cornier when I write it out.)

GLIMMER

BACK IN THE FRIGHT ZONE, if you told me I'd become friends with a princess, I would have wrestled you. But Glimmer is a brave fighter and a great leader, and I'm proud to call her my friend.

THE MOONSTONE

KINGDOM: Bright Moon

RUNESTONE: The Moonstone

WEAPONS AND ACCESSORIES: She carries the magical staff that her dad, Micah, used to use in battle.

POWERS: Glimmer's main power is teleporting. And it's amazing when she hurls energy blasts and sparkle bombs at her attackers. Her powers are connected to the Moonstone.

FAMILY: Her mom is Queen Angella of Bright Moon. Her dad, King Micah, was a powerful sorcerer from Mystacor who died fighting the Horde. Her aunt Castaspella is a sorceress who lives in Mystacor.

LIKES: Leading the Rebellion; sneaking out of her room so she can hang out with me and Bow

DISLIKES: Cleaning her room; when she's far from Bright Moon and she runs out of power, because she's too far from the Moonstone

FAVORITE QUOTE: "No princess left behind!"

GLIMMER'S ROOM

WHEN I FIRST MET GLIMMER, I thought her room in the castle would be filled with frilly princess stuff. And while it is kind of frilly, it's the perfect quarters for the leader of the Rebellion.

Glimmer's bed reminds me of a bird's nest in a tree. She can teleport up to her bed, but if her friends want to hang with her there, we need to climb up these steps.

SOMETIMES GLIMMER HAS TO GET DRESSED UP FOR OFFICIAL PRINCESS FUNCTIONS.

GLIMMER USES THE TARGETS TO PRACTICE HER SPARKLE BLASTS.

I LOVE MY FRIENDS!

Glimmer's lucky that Bow can't stand messes, because he usually cleans up after her.

BOW

BOW WAS NICE TO ME right from the start, even though he thought I was his enemy. That's just the kind of person he is.

KINGDOM: Bright Moon

WEAPONS AND ACCESSORIES: Bow designs trick arrows that he shoots from a collapsible bow. He's a great inventor. He built a tracker pad that can detect magic, First Ones tech, and Horde signals.

POWERS: Bow doesn't have any magic powers, like a princess or a sorcerer would. But I don't think he needs them. He's really skilled with any weapon you put in his hands.

FAMILY: Bow's dads take care of the library in the Whispering Woods. They are fascinated with First Ones tech, which is probably why Bow is so good at figuring it out. He has twelve older siblings who are all historians.

LIKES: Technology; fighting with the Rebellion; hanging out with Glimmer

DISLIKES: The Horde; arguing with Glimmer

FAVORITE QUOTE: "Best Friend Squad to the rescue!"

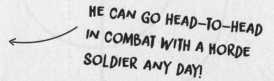
HE CAN GO HEAD-TO-HEAD IN COMBAT WITH A HORDE SOLDIER ANY DAY!

BOW'S ♥ TRICK ARROWS

BOW'S TRICK ARROWS ARE very impressive. He always seems to have the right arrow for just the right situation. Here are a few of them:

LASSO ARROW: A rope uncoils in midair and wraps around whatever Bow is aiming at.

NET ARROW: When Bow shoots the arrow, a chamber opens up and releases a net that surrounds his opponent.

WOW!!

SLIME ARROW: I'm still not exactly sure what this one is for, but it's awesomely gross.

STUN ARROW: Can freeze an enemy in its tracks.

FLARE ARROW: Lights up.

SONIC ARROW: This arrow makes a loud, booming noise when it lands.

BOW'S TRACKER PAD

Bow's invention helps us track down First Ones tech and find our bearings when we're lost. It can also warn us when the Horde is nearby. Bow is always making improvements to it.

BEST FRIEND SQUAD!

ME

GLIMMER

BOW

BEST EVER!

SWIFT WIND

ADORA'S JOURNAL

I know "Best Friend Squad" could sound corny to some people. But when you break it down, it's all true. We are a squad. We work together and each one of us brings different strengths to the team.

And we're also friends—best friends. We like and respect each other, and we accept each other for who we are. The good and the bad.

Catra was my best friend for a long time. At least, I thought she was. But when I became She-Ra she couldn't accept me for who I was—and what I now stood for. She didn't want to believe the truth—that the Horde are really the bad guys. They're the ones hurting Etheria, not the princesses.

Because Catra couldn't accept that, she became my enemy. That was her choice. Not mine.

SWIFT WIND

WHEN I FIRST MET SWIFT WIND, he was an ordinary brown horse who helped me, Glimmer, and Bow escape from the Horde. Then beams from the runestone on my sword accidentally transformed him into a flying, talking horse with a golden horn and rainbow wings.

ME TRANSFORMING SWIFT WIND!

KINGDOM: Bright Moon

POWERS: Swift Wind can talk and fly. He also has the ability to sense when danger is near. When his horn glows, he can connect to the Crystal Castle.

FAMILY: I'm not sure if Swift Wind had a family in the village before he transformed. If he did, he never talks about them. I guess Glimmer, Bow, and I are his family now.

LIKES: Apples; revolution; being part of the Rebellion

DISLIKES: When humans don't take him seriously because he is a horse; not having a chair in the Bright Moon War Room

FAVORITE QUOTE: "I named myself Swift Wind for the swift winds of revolution, because other horses aren't free!"

SO AMAZING!

REPORT:
THE KINGDOM
OF BRIGHT MOON

BRIGHT MOON is the ruling kingdom at the heart of Etheria. It is home to Queen Angella's castle and is surrounded by the Whispering Woods. The Horde has been trying to conquer Bright Moon for decades, with no success.

THE MOONSTONE

MOST PRINCESSES GET THEIR magic from a runestone, a magical stone that is somehow related to the First Ones. The Moonstone is a very big stone that is kept on top of a tall tower outside the royal castle. Queen Angella and Glimmer both get their powers from the Moonstone.

THE MOONSTONE IS SO BEAUTIFUL!

QUEEN ANGELLA

Queen Angella can use the power of the Moonstone to cast a protective shield over Bright Moon. That's why protecting this runestone from the Horde is so important!

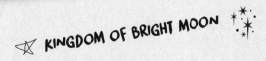
KINGDOM OF BRIGHT MOON

QUEEN ANGELLA

GLIMMER'S MOTHER, QUEEN ANGELLA, once gave up on the Princess Alliance. But now she's the heart of the Rebellion once again. Not only has she been really kind to me, but she's got incredible powers!

KINGDOM: Bright Moon

WEAPONS AND ACCESSORIES: I have never seen her use a weapon except her powers. But she does have amazing wings.

POWERS: Queen Angella can fly. She can also create powerful magical blasts—more powerful than anything I've seen Glimmer do yet. Oh, and she's also immortal!

FAMILY: She is Glimmer's mother, and was married to King Micah. I know that she feels guilty because her husband died in a battle against the Horde that she ordered. I think maybe that's why she is so overprotective of Glimmer.

LIKES: Peace, calm, and beauty

DISLIKES: When Glimmer is in danger

FAVORITE QUOTE: "Glimmer, go to your room!"

KING MICAH

MURAL OF KING MICAH

Glimmer's father was a sorcerer who grew up in the kingdom of Mystacor. But even the powerful magic he learned there could not save him from the Horde.

BRIGHT MOON GUARDS

BRIGHT MOON IS PROTECTED BY guards who are under the command of Queen Angella. They take their task seriously, and they look really mysterious. Like you wouldn't want to mess with them. But I wish Queen Angella would let me fix their uniforms just a little bit.

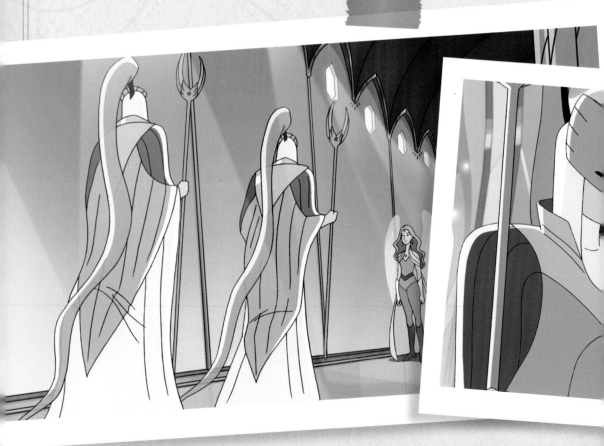

These long, flowing robes are beautiful, but can you run fast in them? I vote for pants.

Bright Moon guards are the best in Etheria! They don't need to run fast, because the Horde runs from <u>them</u>. —G

HI, GLIMMER!

Maybe these staffs could do more damage if the points were facing out, and not in.

THESE MASKS HAVE TO IMPAIR THEIR VISION, RIGHT?

THINGS BRIGHT MOON HAS THAT
I NEVER KNEW EXISTED

1. **SOFT PILLOWS:** The beds in the Horde barracks are as hard as rocks, and the pillows might as well be bricks. Even the blankets here are soft, and not scratchy!

2. **HORSES:** Pretty much the only animals in the Horde are creepy-crawly bugs. I was shocked to see cute, fluffy bunnies, and even more shocked when I first met Swift Wind. Horses are so beautiful and majestic! Riding Swift Wind beats riding a skiff any day.

3. **PARTIES:** Before I came here, I had heard of a search party and a scouting party. But here, a "party" is when a bunch of people get together and listen to music and eat food and talk. Can you imagine? Nobody even gives out any orders, unless you count when Bow says, "Everybody dance!"

4. **HOT SHOWERS:** They actually heat the water here when they wash themselves.

5. ICE CREAM: When they have parties, they serve this thing called ice cream, which is cold and creamy and tastes sweet (new word I learned). Bow says that's because it's made with honey, which is apparently something that bees make. That sounds gross, I know, but it tastes really good. And get this: Sometimes they even have ice cream when there is no party!

6. FRUITS AND VEGETABLES: They are not as tasty as ice cream but they still taste pretty good. Swift Wind tells me that they grow out of the ground. I had no idea. In the Fright Zone, all we eat are ration bars that come from the factory. I never knew there might be other things to eat.

PRINCESS FROSTA'S ICE CREAM SUNDAE

Since I am practically an ice cream expert, I asked Adora if I could include a recipe in her book and she said yes. So here's how to make my favorite sundae, which tastes like winter, the very best season!

1. Start with a scoop of pink or green peppermint ice cream.

2. Top it with whipped cream and crushed-up peppermint candy.

3. Finish it with pink and white sprinkles.

PRINCESS FROSTA ♡

35

♡ BRIGHT MOON IS THE BEST!

When I first came to Bright Moon, I didn't think I would ever fit in. It was so sunny, and colorful, and . . . nice. And even though I was a princess, I had been a Horde soldier all of my life. Tough. Strong. I didn't need fun, or parties, or ice cream.

I thought I would have to change who I was to fit in. But pretty soon I realized something. Princesses are tough and strong, too. Maybe I don't know how to dance or what to wear to a party, but those things aren't important. Deep down, we all have a lot in common.

I also learned that the best way to fit in is to show that you care about Bright Moon. To show that you will protect it and are willing to fight for it. And for me, that's easy to do. Even easier than getting dressed up.

REPORT:
THE PRINCESSES
OF ETHERIA

GLIMMER AND QUEEN ANGELLA aren't the only ones with magical powers. There are princesses all over Etheria. Each one is in charge of her own kingdom. Each one has her own special power. In this section of my report, I've outlined key information about each one of them.

The first time we all fought side by side together, in the battle of Bright Moon, we learned something important. When we combine our powers, we are stronger than ever. That's why princesses have to stick together!

MERMISTA

WHEN I FIRST MET MERMISTA, I thought she didn't care about fighting the Horde, but she proved me wrong. She has come to She-Ra's rescue more than once!

Kingdom: Salineas

Runestone: The Pearl

Weapons and Accessories: Her royal trident

Powers: Her legs can transform into a mermaid tail, and she can control water. I've seen her blast opponents with ocean waves, and pummel them with bubbles.

Family: Her father used to control the Salineas Sea Gate, but she took it over after he retired.

Likes: Protecting her kingdom

Dislikes: Group hugs

Favorite Quote: "This is how it's done in the sea!"

SPLASH, SPLASH!

THE KINGDOM OF SALINEAS

THIS KINGDOM SITS IN THE middle of the ocean. Tall purple towers spiral above the waves. Protecting the kingdom is the Sea Gate, a massive wall of First Ones technology that prevents intruders from getting into Salineas. Princess Mermista can open and close the gate using her royal trident.

The only way to get
to Salineas is by boat.
The nearest land is a
seaport town called
Seaworthy. It's a haven
for misfits and pirates.

FROSTA

I GOT A FROSTY RECEPTION when I first met Frosta, because I pointed out that she was just a kid. But I quickly learned that she is way more powerful than her size. And when we're not sure what to do, she always has lots of good ideas.

BRRRR!!

LOOK AT HER GO!

KINGDOM: The Kingdom of Snows

RUNESTONE: The Fractal Flake

POWERS: Frosta is always thinking up new ways to use her powers. She can shoot ice from her hands, create icicle spikes that rise up from the floor, make ice cannonballs, and cover herself in ice armor. When she joins forces with Mermista, she can freeze all of Mermista's water attacks. But her coolest power is the Ice Hammer. That's when she transforms her fist into a hammer of ice, and smashes away!

LIKES: Fighting side by side with Glimmer

DISLIKES: When people don't respect her because of her age

FAVORITE QUOTE: "*Ice* of you to drop in!"

THE KINGDOM OF SNOWS

THE LARGEST AND MOST POWERFUL kingdom in Etheria has been safe from evil for centuries. It's in a remote location, far from the Horde. Frosta's palace, Castle Evernight, is on a high mountain peak that rises into the clouds. The cold, frozen terrain is a challenge for invading troops.

THIS FOOD WAS AMAZING!

Because the Kingdom of Snows was so safe, Princess Frosta didn't think she needed to join the Rebellion. But when the Horde invaded a party at the palace (the Princess Prom), Frosta agreed to join the fight.

FROSTA'S SNOW GUARDS PROTECT THE CASTLE—AND ALSO SERVE FOOD AT HER PARTIES.

SO PRETTY!

PERFUMA

PEACE-LOVING PERFUMA used to think she wasn't strong enough to face the Horde. But when she joined the Rebellion, she learned that she was much more powerful than she ever thought.

KINGDOM: Plumeria

RUNESTONE: The Heart-Blossom

WEAPONS AND ACCESSORIES: Perfuma is not into weapons. She can make flower crowns for herself and her friends, but they're not useful in a battle situation.

POWERS: She can control and grow plants and flowers. I've seen her make lightning-fast vines that wrap around her opponents. But her most awesome creation is a Plant Golem—a giant creature made of plants!

LIKES: Peace, love, and harmony

DISLIKES: Anything that messes with peace, love, and harmony. You can tell when that's happening when her eye twitches.

FAVORITE QUOTE: "Maybe we should hold hands and think healing thoughts."

JUST THE
SWEETEST!

THE KINGDOM OF PLUMERIA

THE PEOPLE OF PERFUMA'S KINGDOM have lived in tranquility for a thousand years. Plumeria is known for its beautiful flowers and majestic trees.

HOW COOL IS THIS?

Perfuma's runestone, the Heart-Blossom, is embedded in the trunk of an enormous tree with pink leaves. Perfuma gets her power from the Heart-Blossom, and its energy helps make everything grow in Plumeria.

DON'T MESS WITH THESE GUYS!

The inhabitants of Plumeria are as peace-loving as Perfuma. But when the Horde poisoned their land, they joined the fight with us.

NETOSSA

I HAVE NEVER SEEN Netossa without Spinnerella. These are two princesses I know I can always count on!

KINGDOM: She has never been tied to a specific kingdom, but she's always been willing to help the Rebellion.

RUNESTONE: None

POWERS: Netossa can conjure up magical energy nets that she can use to trap objects and opponents, big and small.

LIKES: Taking down the Horde

DISLIKES: When people underestimate her powers

FAVORITE QUOTE: "Nets. I toss nets. Okay?"

SPINNERELLA

SOMETIMES SPINNERELLA REMINDS me of a calm, gentle breeze. But when we're facing the Horde, she can whip up a mighty storm of power.

KINGDOM: Like Netossa, she's not tied to a specific kingdom. But she's always been an ally to the Rebellion.

RUNESTONE: None

POWERS: Spinnerella commands the power of wind. When she spins, she creates whirling cyclones that blow away her enemies.

LIKES: The color purple; being in the heart of the action

DISLIKES: Waiting for something to happen. She'd rather make things happen.

FAVORITE QUOTE: "Princesses stick together!" YEAH!!

ENTRAPTA

ENTRAPTA IS A BRILLIANT INVENTOR, and I sometimes think she cares more about machines than people. ~~But she risked her life to help us when the Horde captured Glimmer and Bow, and we lost her that day. We will never forget her.~~

ENTRAPTA IS ALIVE, AND WORKING FOR THE HORDE! HOW? WHY? I JUST DON'T UNDERSTAND!

KINGDOM: ~~Dryl~~ *NOW SHE LIVES IN THE FRIGHT ZONE*

RUNESTONE: None

WEAPONS AND ACCESSORIES: Emily, a Horde robot that she reprogrammed to be her pet.

POWERS: Entrapta can use the strands of her long hair like they're extra arms, hands, and even legs. But her strongest power is her tech ability. She really is a genius!

LIKES: Robots, machines, tiny food, and fizzy beverages

DISLIKES: Having to interact with people

FAVORITE QUOTE: "I'm on the side of science!"

Entrapta created Emily, her reprogrammed Horde robot, when we infiltrated the Fright Zone. She was really interested in all of the Horde technology there.

THAT'S EMILY . . .
CUTE, RIGHT?

THE KINGDOM OF DRYL

OTHER KINGDOMS IN ETHERIA are filled with people, but when Glimmer, Bow, and I first saw Dryl, it was mostly deserted. Entrapta had a few humans in her castle who prepared her food, but she created a small army of robots to do everything else for her.

Entrapta also designed Crypto Castle herself. It's an elaborate maze that only she can get around. She added lots of booby traps to protect it from intruders.

Crypto Castle is a pretty impressive place, but all it took was one mysterious piece of First Ones tech to infect the robots with a virus, which turned them into unstoppable killers. Well, almost unstoppable. One of Bow's trick arrows helped destroy the tech and save the castle.

UGH, SO CREEPY

REPORT: FRIENDS OF THE REBELLION

IF THE REBELLION IS GOING TO SUCCEED and take down Hordak once and for all, we will need all the help we can get. Luckily, other people have stepped up to join us—everyone from ordinary villagers to a tough-as-nails warrior.

In this section of my report, I've outlined some of the other key members of the Rebellion.

CASTASPELLA

GLIMMER'S AUNT IS THE HEAD sorceress of Mystacor. She's a big help to the Rebellion, but she can be so weird with Glimmer sometimes. She loves Glimmer, but she's always hinting that Glimmer should change things about herself.

Personally, I think Glimmer is perfect just the way she is.

Aw, thanks Adora! <3 -G

KINGDOM: Mystacor

RUNESTONE: None. Sorcerers don't use runestones to create magic.

FAMILY: She is King Micah's sister, which makes her Glimmer's aunt.

POWERS: She casts awesome spells. I've seen her create illusions, and make things move through the air.

LIKES: Knitting sweaters and socks; when Glimmer comes to visit

DISLIKES: Anything that is a threat to Mystacor

FAVORITE QUOTE: "Don't you want to spend more time with your aunt?"

THE KINGDOM OF MYSTACOR

THE SORCERERS OF ETHERIA train here, a hidden kingdom that floats in the clouds. When Glimmer, Bow, and I visited there, I saw some pretty amazing things:

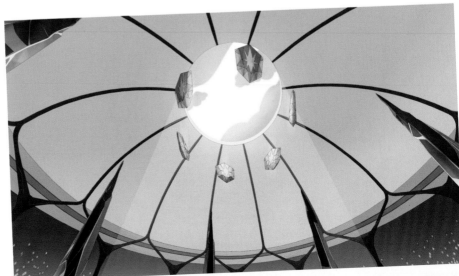

1. **THE LUNAR LENSES**: The sorcerers cast an invisibility spell on Mystacor so that no evil can find it. They use the Lunar Lens to recharge the spell.

2. **THE HALL OF SORCERERS**: There's a statue of Glimmer's dad, Micah, here.

3. **THE STEAM GROTTO**: An underground cave with pools of bubbling, warm water. Glimmer says it's supposed to be relaxing.

It IS relaxing! One of these days you will learn how to chill, Adora. -G

I DON'T GET IT . . .

THE DIFFERENCES BETWEEN PRINCESSES AND SORCERERS

IT TOOK ME A WHILE to figure out the differences between princesses and sorcerers. They can both do magic, but their magic comes from different sources.

PRINCESSES

- Princesses usually get their powers from a runestone.
- They have different powers that are all related to each other, like Frosta's ice powers or Perfuma's plant powers.
- A princess can lose her power if the runestone is destroyed.

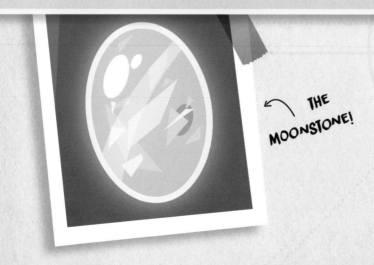

THE MOONSTONE!

SORCERERS

- Sorcerers are usually born with some magical ability.
- They can learn to channel their powers by drawing magical runes and symbols to cast spells.
- Because they're born with their powers, they can never really lose them.
- Sorcerers who use their powers for darkness instead of light will be banished from Mystacor. That explains what happened to Shadow Weaver.

SEA HAWK

SEA HAWK'S PIRATE SKILLS can come in handy, if you can get him to stop bragging, singing shanties, and talking about "derring-do"—whatever that is.

HE LOVES FIRE!

KINGDOM: I first met Sea Hawk in the town of Seaworthy, but I'm not sure if he lives there. He seems to travel around a lot.

WEAPONS AND ACCESSORIES: You might say that his mustache is an accessory.

POWERS: Sea Hawk doesn't have any magical powers, but he's a master sailor and is always up for adventure.

LIKES: Princess Mermista, his "close personal friend"; setting his ship on fire

DISLIKES: Losing to me in arm wrestling

FAVORITE QUOTE: "Forward to adventure!"

HAHA!

SEA HAWK'S SEA SHANTY

I'm Sea Hawk. I am, I am!

If you're looking for adventure, then I am your man!

If you want to ride on the waves through the deepest blue,

Through perilous winds, then I've got you.

Some say I'm a hero,

Some say I'm a man.

What I know for sure is:

I'm Sea Hawk. I am, I am!

I'm Sea Hawk. I am, I am!

MADAME RAZZ

MADAME RAZZ MIGHT BE THE most mysterious person I've ever encountered. I first met her in the Whispering Woods, right after I became She-Ra. She kept calling me "Mara," and it was a long time before I knew what she was talking about.

KINGDOM: She lives in the Whispering Woods outside of Bright Moon.

WEAPONS AND ACCESSORIES: I've seen her use her broom to pummel a Horde soldier. And wherever she goes, moths flutter around her.

POWERS: I honestly am not sure if she's magical or not. She's definitely not an ordinary old lady. I've seen her climb up the beacon like a mountain goat, and she can run faster than I can!

LIKES: Picking berries

DISLIKES: When the Princess Alliance broke up

FAVORITE QUOTE: "I don't have my glasses. You have to speak up!"

MARA

I'm learning more and more about Mara, but it's still so confusing. She was She-Ra before I was, a long time ago. It looks like something really bad might have happened when she was She-Ra, but I'm not exactly sure what it was . . . or if the same thing could happen to me.

← HOLOGRAM OF MARA

HUNTARA

HUNTARA IS THE NEWEST ADDITION to the Rebellion. She's a trained Horde soldier, just like I am. She spent a long time hiding out from the Horde, and I'm really glad she's on our side.

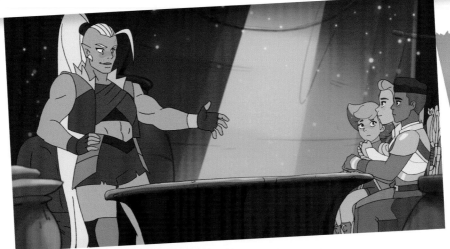

KINGDOM: When I first met her, she was the unofficial leader of the Crimson Waste, which isn't a kingdom, exactly. It's more like a wild land where anything goes. Before that, she lived in the Fright Zone.

WEAPONS AND ACCESSORIES: She has an amazing extending spear.

POWERS: Besides being a skilled and powerful fighter, she's an expert tracker.

LIKES: A good fight

DISLIKES: Disloyalty

FAVORITE QUOTE: "What I saw in the Horde scared me, and I ran. But I'm not going to run anymore!"

REPORT:
THE HORDE

THE HORDE IS A THREAT to the people of Etheria. They have armies of trained soldiers, high-tech robots, and sophisticated weapons at their disposal. They believe all princesses are evil and want to destroy them.

I know all this because I used to be a Horde soldier. I know how dangerous they are, and how much they want to rule Etheria. This gives me an advantage, because the best way to defeat your enemy is to know them.

CATRA

CATRA . . . IT STILL HURTS to think that we used to be best friends, and to see what she's become. She is so full of anger and hate. I used to think there was some way to get through to her, to get her to join the Rebellion so we could fight the Horde together. But I don't think that will ever happen.

KINGDOM: The Fright Zone

WEAPONS AND ACCESSORIES: Like other Horde soldiers, she uses a stun-baton. Now she also uses a whip she got in the Crimson Waste.

POWERS: She is agile, quick, and strong. She can use her sharp claws as weapons, too.

LIKES: Doing the wrong thing, because it's fun

DISLIKES: Water

FAVORITE QUOTE: "It's time to show those princesses a thing or two."

I MISS YOU, CATRA

MY OLD TEAMMATES

CADETS IN THE HORDE are assigned to training teams that compete against each other. You sleep, eat, and train with your teammates, which means you get pretty close. I was on a team with Catra, Lonnie, Rogelio, and Kyle.

LONNIE

She talks a big game, but she's got the skills to back it up. She takes being a Horde soldier very seriously, and she's really competitive.

ROGELIO

Even though he doesn't talk, I never had a problem understanding Rogelio. He was up for any task, and gives everything all he's got.

KYLE

I think Kyle is his own worst enemy! He could be a good soldier, but he has no self-confidence. He expects to fail, so he usually does.

SCORPIA

SCORPIA IS A FORCE CAPTAIN. I didn't know her that well when I was in the Horde. Then she started hanging out with Catra, and I got to see her in action. I can't figure her out. She seems kind of goofy and nice, but she's totally loyal to Hordak and the Horde.

KINGDOM: She lives in the Fright Zone, but she was born a princess of the Scorpion Kingdom. That's right—she's a princess! When the Scorpion Kingdom joined forces with Hordak, they turned over the Black Garnet runestone. That means that Scorpia doesn't get to access its powers. Instead, Hordak lets Shadow Weaver use it.

WEAPONS AND ACCESSORIES: She doesn't need weapons, because her scorpion tail is full of poison. Her attacks have a real sting!

POWERS: She's really strong—almost as strong as She-Ra!

LIKES: Catra. It's like she's Catra's new best friend, or something.

DISLIKES: Being alone

FAVORITE QUOTE: "Just so you know, I'm a hugger."

SHADOW WEAVER

I USED TO THINK THAT Shadow Weaver cared about me—until I found out that everything she had ever told me was a lie. It looks like Catra took her place as Hordak's favorite. I'm pretty sure she's not too happy about that!

KINGDOM: The Fright Zone, but she was once a sorcery teacher in Mystacor—before she embarked on a dark path that led her to Hordak.

WEAPONS AND ACCESSORIES: Shadow Weaver uses the Black Garnet runestone to give power to her sorcery. In theory, this makes her more powerful than any princess. She always wears a mask over her face, and nobody is sure what is underneath.

POWERS: She can control shadows and create shadow spies that do her bidding.

LIKES: Power

DISLIKES: Being disobeyed

FAVORITE QUOTE: "Do not disappoint me!"

LIGHT SPINNER

Before she became Shadow Weaver, she was known as Light Spinner, a powerful sorcerer of Mystacor. Castaspella told me that Light Spinner was cast out of Mystacor because she sought power and control above all other things. That sounds like Shadow Weaver to me!

← **STATUE OF LIGHT SPINNER**

HORDAK

BOO!!

EVEN THOUGH I GREW UP in the Horde, I don't know much about Hordak. He usually stays in the shadows, working on his inventions. What I mostly know about him is this:
He wants to rule Etheria,
and he doesn't care who or
what he destroys to do it.

KINGDOM: The Fright Zone

WEAPONS AND ACCESSORIES: He wears armor and a big cape all the time; but yeah, I think that's his real face, and not a mask.

POWERS: He has good tech skills, and he's really good at ordering people around.

LIKES: Being in charge

DISLIKES: When anybody questions him or stands up to him

FAVORITE QUOTE: "Our mission is to destroy the princesses and their ridiculous Rebellion!"

HORDAK'S SIDEKICK

Hordak's creepy little pet, Imp,
is also his spy. Keep an eye out
for him, because he reports
everything he sees to Hordak!

THE FRIGHT ZONE

I'VE SPENT MOST OF MY life inside the walls of the Fright Zone. It's a dark, crowded, sprawling compound of metal buildings, spiraling towers, and factories spewing smoke into the red sky. Almost everything you see there was designed for the sole purpose of building an army capable of defeating the princesses.

THE WEAPONS FOUNDRY: Where the weapons used by the Horde are created, including spears, laser cannons, and stun-batons

THE VEHICLE BAY: Storage for skiffs, tanks, and other Horde vehicles

THE BARRACKS: Sleeping quarters for soldiers, cadets, and factory workers

THE COMMISSARY: Where every Fright Zone resident receives their daily allocation of ration bars. Soldiers are lucky—they get an extra one.

HORDAK'S LAB: All of the Horde's weapons, robots, and technology start with ideas that Hordak comes up with in his lab. There's normally a lot of lightning, sparks, and strange sounds that come from here.

THE ROBOT BAY: Storage for the Horde Bots

HORDE TECHNOLOGY

THIS IS THE TECHNOLOGY I was trained to operate when I was a Horde cadet—but they are coming up with new tech all the time.

Thanks to Entrapta's help! This is bad news for the Rebellion!!

SKIFF: This is a speedy vehicle that hovers a few feet over the ground. Easy to maneuver around trees and buildings. They are lightweight, though, and easy to take down with a simple blast from just about any weapon.

STUN-BATON: Every Horde soldier carries one of these. It delivers a powerful shock that can paralyze any opponent. When facing a Horde soldier, try to disarm their stun-baton before doing anything else.

HORDE BOT: These walking robots do not need to be operated by a soldier, which is an advantage for the Horde. Until recently, they were easy to take down with a shot to the laser eye, but new robots are able to repair themselves instantly.

THINGS I MISS ABOUT THE HORDE

1. I miss the rigid schedule. It never changed, and I always knew what to expect.

2. I miss the constant sound of machines whirring. In Bright Moon, there's always music playing, or people laughing, and birds singing. It's nice but it makes it hard to focus!

3. Believe it or not, I miss my hard cot in the barracks. My bed in the castle is way too soft!

4. Catra . . . sometimes.

CATRA

THINGS I DO NOT MISS ABOUT THE HORDE

1. Ration bars. Ice cream is just so much better. And just about anything else I've eaten in Bright Moon. ♡

2. That smell in the air. The Fright Zone smells like . . . burning metal. Bright Moon smells like flowers and sunshine.

3. The morning wake-up siren. It's much nicer to wake up to the sound of birds chirping.

4. Freezing cold showers

BRIGHT MOON IS SO PLEASANT!

91

ME AND MY SWORD ♡

Sometimes at night I can't fall asleep. The same thought keeps running through my head.

Why didn't I realize that the Horde was evil?

I believed everything I was taught. That princesses were the real evil. That we had to destroy them to save Etheria. I believed that when the Horde was attacking villages, they were taking down evil armies—not innocent people.

I imagine what my life would have been like if I hadn't found the sword. As force captain, I would have led troops into those villages. I would have decimated homes and innocent lives with the Horde's powerful weapons . . .

"Adora, you are a good person at heart," Glimmer told me when I shared this with her. "You would have figured it out on your own. And anyway, it didn't take long for you to see the truth. Some people never see it."

I knew she was talking about Catra. Maybe it's too late for her. But I know there are other good people in the Horde. People just like me, who don't realize they're being lied to.

If I can change, maybe they can, too.

REPORT:
SHE-RA AND THE FIRST ONES

EVER SINCE I FOUND THE SWORD, I have been trying to figure out what it means to be She-Ra. I know that she is tied to the First Ones, the people who lived on Etheria more than a thousand years ago. There are First Ones ruins all over the planet, and exploring them has been the best way for me to learn more about She-Ra—and why I was chosen to be her.

THE LEGEND OF SHE-RA

A long time ago, the First Ones came from beyond the stars. They settled Etheria and used their technology to protect it.

Now the princesses protect the planet when they are in balance. Their runestones are connected to them, to the planet, and to other runestones.

But it is the purpose of one princess, She-Ra, to protect all of Etheria. Legend says that when Etheria is threatened, She-Ra will appear to save it. She-Ra is Etheria's champion, appointed by the First Ones to protect and unite the planet.

The last She-Ra, Mara, appeared one thousand years ago.

I am the first new She-Ra in all of that time. It is my job to save Etheria from the Horde.

But what if I can't?

LIGHT HOPE

SHE-RA IS SUPPOSED TO be able to heal, and to protect. But when I first became She-Ra, I had no idea how to use my powers. I needed help.

Then I met Madame Razz in the woods, and she led me to the Beacon, a First Ones ruin. Inside, I found a chamber: the Crystal Castle. There, Light Hope appeared to me. She's a hologram.

The First Ones created Light Hope to watch over Etheria. She knows all about She-Ra and my powers and she helps me train. But she's a computer program, not a human, so she doesn't always have an answer to my questions.

THE CRYSTAL CASTLE

Light Hope's holographic chamber is beautiful, a room with no walls and constantly shifting rainbow crystals. She can transform it into a training ground for me, or project my memories onto the crystals.

FIRST ONES
LANGUAGE PRIMER

When I see First Ones language, the meanings of the words just pop up in my head. I've been working with Bow's dads to try to write instructions for how to read it. It's kind of complicated, but we figured out that there are a few basic rules:

1. Instead of letters, the language uses symbols that stand for different sounds.

2. The language goes right to left, not left to right.

3. Each word in the language is a line, or a branch. The syllables of the word are stems that are connected to each other below the branch.

4. To read a word, start by reading the symbol on the right, and move left.

THE ALPHABET

The alphabet is phonetic.

CONSONANTS

B ◇	CH ◺	D ◉	DH ▽				
F ▽	G ◈	H ■	J ◹				
K ◇	L ▱	M ◆	N ●				
NG ▼	P ◇	R ▱	S △				
SH ▽	T □	TH ◭	V ▽				
W △	Z △	ZH ▽					

VOWELS

SAD   ALL   SAY

○○   ○   ▲   ▌

PET   FEET   LIT   I

〉   ●●   ⊙

GOOD   TOO   GO

HOUSE   FUN   BOY   YES

101

FIRST ONES LANGUAGE PRACTICE

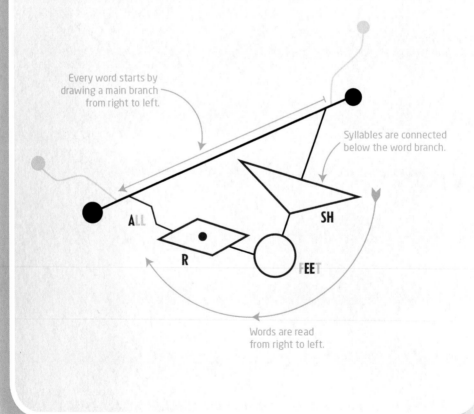

① **WORD BRANCH & SYLLABLES**
"SHE-RA"

Every word starts by drawing a main branch from right to left.

Syllables are connected below the word branch.

ALL

SH

R

FEET

Words are read from right to left.

Reading the language is easy for me—but writing it is a whole different thing! I've been practicing with a few names.

② DOTS & STEMS
"SCORPIA"

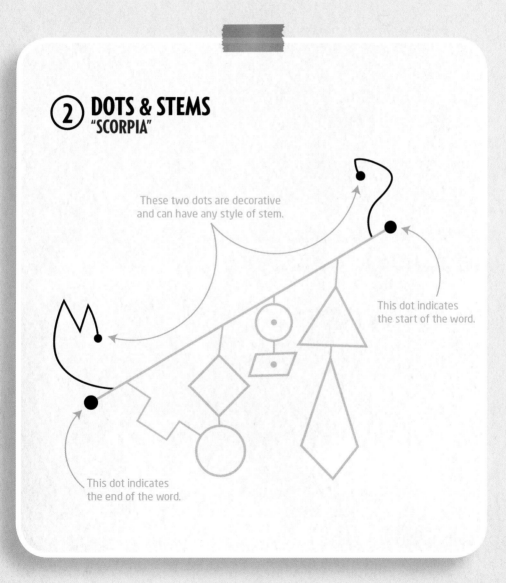

These two dots are decorative and can have any style of stem.

This dot indicates the start of the word.

This dot indicates the end of the word.

FIRST ONES TECH

EVEN THOUGH THE FIRST ONES lived on Etheria more than a thousand years ago, their technology is way more advanced than ours. Bow's tracker helps him find First Ones tech, and now I know that Entrapta's experiments with First Ones technology affected runestones.

This is one piece of First Ones tech I definitely don't like. If it makes contact with my runestone, it infects it, and turns She-Ra into a chaotic monster that I can't control. I've seen it infect Elementals, too. Luckily, Scorpia destroyed it—but I hope there aren't any more of them out there.

ELEMENTALS

MAYBE SOME OF THE GREATEST examples of First Ones tech are creatures called the Elementals. They are enormous, bug-like beasts with dangerous speed and sharp teeth.

Elementals are only found at First Ones sites. The First Ones created them to protect the sites, so they don't activate unless an intruder appears. When I transform into She-Ra, they immediately stop attacking. But when they're infected, nothing stops them.

My memories of being infected with the First One tech are pretty fuzzy, but I do remember the pure, raw rage I felt. I remember the feeling that I wanted to destroy everything around me—even my friends.

It makes me wonder if that's what happened to Mara. Light Hope says that she couldn't control her power, and that it became too much for her mind. That her actions led to devastation. "She gave into fear," Light Hope said.

What if that happens to me? I am afraid of my powers, sometimes, too. Will I snap, like Mara did? Will I hurt people I love?

It's a terrifying thought. And sometimes I think it's not fair. I didn't ask to be She-Ra. I bet Mara didn't, either. But I am She-Ra, and I've got to do my best to keep it together.

It's too scary to think about what might happen if I don't.

REPORT:
OTHER LOCATIONS IN ETHERIA

UNTIL I BECAME SHE-RA, the only place I ever knew was the Fright Zone. But in a short time, I've traveled all over Etheria, to far-off kingdoms, and remote outposts. I've seen some beautiful sights, and some spooky things, too.

I've reported on the kingdoms already. Here is some information about some other key places in Etheria.

THE WHISPERING WOODS

IN THE HORDE, CADETS ARE WARNED never to travel into the Whispering Woods. If you do, they say, you will never return.

The woods surround the Fright Zone and passing through them is the only way to get to Bright Moon. I've traveled through them many times since I left the Horde, and I've made it out. But I understand how the rumors started.

KEY SPOTS IN THE WOODS

In these woods, you'll find Madame Razz's cabin, the Beacon, and the library run by Bow's dads. It's packed with First Ones books and artifacts.

It's easy to get lost in the woods. The land is constantly shifting, so you might be aiming for one place but end up in a completely different place. I think the First Ones made this happen to protect the location of their sites. That's the same reason they created the Elementals: to protect their buildings and technology. I've always wondered—what exactly were they protecting themselves from?

OTHER LOCATIONS

THE NORTHERN REACH: This frozen outpost is nothing but snow and ice. One good thing about being She-Ra here is that I don't need to wear a coat! She-Ra doesn't feel the cold.

ALWYN, THE HAUNTED OUTPOST: I visited this deserted out post with Bow, Glimmer, and Swift Wind. The farmers deserted the village, claiming it was haunted by ghosts. We didn't find any ghosts—but we found a First Ones communications hub where they projected messages to their loved ones.

BEAST ISLAND: I've never been to Beast Island. I'm not even sure if it's real. In the Horde, it's the place where Hordak threatens to send anyone who disobeys him. Terrifying beasts are supposed to run wild there, so being sent there is basically a death sentence.

THE CRIMSON WASTE

THE CRIMSON WASTE MIGHT BE the most difficult place to survive in all of Etheria. Technology doesn't work there. There are monsters wherever you turn, quicksand around every corner, and even the plants can kill you! The inhabitants there are mainly criminals, who've developed their own society and their own heartless sense of justice.

It's a difficult, lawless place, so it's no surprise that Catra loves it. She's not afraid of anyone or anything there. Good—she can have it. I couldn't wait to get out of there!

MARA'S SPACESHIP

In the Crimson Waste, we found a crashed spaceship.
I knew it was Mara's spaceship. Inside, there was a
holographic message from Mara for the future She-Ra.
That's when I learned for sure that Mara had turned
against the First Ones. But she hadn't been trying to
destroy Etheria—she was trying to save it . . .

RANDOM STUFF

IN THIS SECTION, I'M RECORDING some other important things that didn't fit in the other sections. Oh, and Glimmer and Bow discovered that I was writing this book. They told the other princesses, and then they all wanted to add some things they said I forgot. So there's some stuff from them in this section, too. And I mean "stuff," because I wouldn't call them reports, exactly. Princesses are great at magic, but they could definitely use some training in proper report writing!

THE PRINCESS PROM

THE ALL-PRINCESS BALL—AKA PRINCESS PROM— IS A kind of "party"—an event where people get together for the only purpose of having fun. There's dancing and fancy food and everyone puts on frilly clothes. It only happens once every ten years, and all of the princesses are invited.

There are lots of rules about the Princess Prom. Here's just the first page of the invitation:

PRINCESS PROM INVITATION
TABLE OF CONTENTS

I. ATTIRE

II. RULES FOR GREETING THE HOSTESS
    a. Expected Curtsy Depth
    b. Proper Stair Descending Etiquette

III. ACCEPTABLE DEMEANOR
    a. Yawning Procedure (Only in Case of Medical Emergency)
    b. Slouching Protocols

IV. DANCE MOVES
    a. Acceptable
    b. Unacceptable
    c. Required

Continued . . .

I was intimidated until I realized that a party was no different than a military operation. So I prepped the way I normally would:

- I DIVIDED THE RULES INTO BASE PARTS.

- I BROKE DOWN THE BALLROOM INTO FOUR QUADRANTS AND MEMORIZED THE BACKGROUND INFORMATION OF EVERY PRINCESS.

- I MADE A CHART SHOWING THE RELATIONSHIPS BETWEEN THEM ALL: FRIENDS, ENEMIES, AND ENEMIES.

- I EVEN MADE AN OBSTACLE COURSE!

I was prepared for any and all possible scenarios.

PRINCESS PROM PICTURES

Princess Frosta hosted the prom in the Kingdom of Snows.

Entrapta thought the party was a social experiment and showed up to observe human behavior. She was happy that they served lots of tiny food.

Glimmer got jealous when Bow and Perfuma went to the party together.

I was NOT jealous! —G

I *thought* I was prepared for every possible scenario. But I definitely didn't count on Catra and Scorpia showing up.

BOW'S WAR TABLE
BATTLE FIGURES

Bow here! When it comes to strategic planning sessions, Adora is the best. She uses a war table that maps out her target location. But I noticed one thing missing: battle figures! As a member of the Etherian Maker Community, I knew what I had to do. I created custom hand-painted figures—and they came out awesome.

They're dolls! —Mermista

No, they're battle figures!!

Tiny She-Ra! She's small, but she's strong.

Tiny Bow comes with his own tiny arrows.

That's me, Adora, and Glimmer strategizing at the war table.

I'm still trying to figure out a way to make Tiny Glimmer sparkle.

♡ PERFUMA'S GUIDE TO ♡ PERFECT HARMONY

Hi, it's Perfuma! Adora is so wonderful at fighting and strategizing for battle! But when it comes to battling stress, she needs help. Here are my strategies for finding harmony when things around you are . . . not so harmonious.

1. Focus on the positive, not the negative! When the Horde attacks, think about all of the wonderful friends around you who will help you battle them.

2. Take deep breaths and center your mind and body. *How can you take deep breaths when you're running from a Horde robot?*

3. Visualize what you want to achieve! Picture yourself defeating the Horde. *I like this one!*

4. Stop and smell the flowers. Flowers make everything better! *What if the Horde destroys all the flowers?*

5. Trust in the universe! Everything usually works out all right in the end.

I hope you're right!

THE BRIGHT MOON ARMORY

This is Glimmer. Even when my mom was trying to keep me safe and far away from the Rebellion, I knew that Bright Moon would be called on to defend itself one day. So I secretly started collecting weapons for both offense and defense and stashing them in the castle. They came in handy during the Battle of Bright Moon!

FIGHTING STAFF   SHIELD

ARMOR   MACE

ARROWS   SWORD

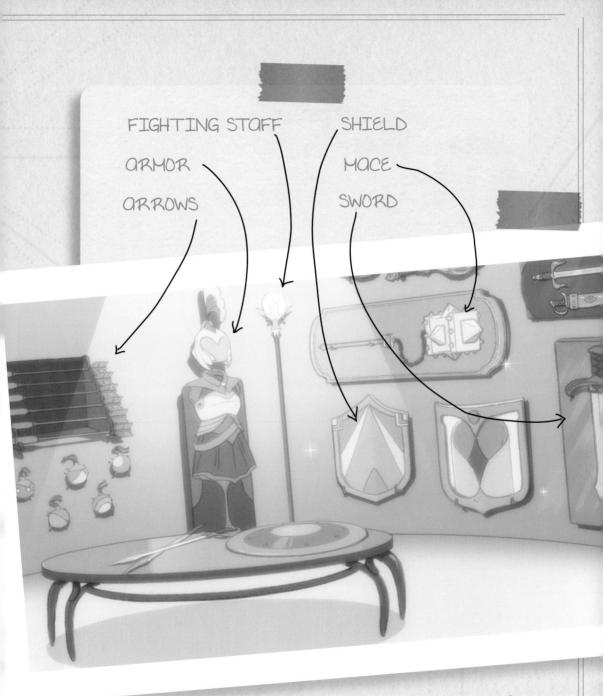

A princess has got to
be prepared for anything!

FREE THE ♡ HORSES!

I, Swift Wind of Bright Moon, hereby dictate this manifesto to Adora because I cannot hold a pen:

As a member of the Rebellion, I am proud to lead the fight against the Horde. But there is another, equally important fight that cannot be ignored: The horses of Etheria are enslaved by their human masters!

I call upon the Princess Alliance to help me free the horses of Etheria! They deserve to run free through the fields and meadows, to feel the wind blowing through their manes.

I have brought this message of rebellion to my comrades in their stables, and so far they have been uninspired to join me. They are content to live on their cozy farms, eating all of the food they want, and being cared for by their owners. But they have no idea what they are missing out on. The sweet taste of freedom is far more delicious than the taste of freshly mown hay!

So I implore you, princesses, help me in this noble mission. FREE THE HORSES OF ETHERIA!

FROSTA'S CODE NAMES FOR THE REBELS

Frosta reporting! I once suggested that every member of the Rebellion should be assigned a code name, to approve efficiency. Nobody liked my idea but I really think the council needs to consider it. Here are my suggestions.

Me: Frostbite

Glimmer: Sparkle Bomb

Perfuma: Flower Power

Mermista: Tidal Wave

Spinnerella: Wind Storm

Netossa: Web Shooter

Bow: Sure Shot

She-Ra: Sword Warrior

Dear Catra,

You are my enemy now, and you always will be. I know that now. All this time, I had hope. Hope that you would see the light. Hope that you would realize that Etheria is a beautiful place that needs to be saved, and not destroyed.

I have no more hope now, and that makes me sad. So sad. Because I miss you, Catra, and I will always miss you.

I miss your smile. I miss the gleam in your eye when you would beat me in a race during training. I miss laughing with you when we would play a prank on one of the other cadets in the barracks. I even miss you snoring in the bunk above me.

Those are the things I remember when I think about you. I'm going to try to remember the good things about you, instead of the bad ones. Because those break my heart.

I'm sorry things ended up like this. I really am. But even if we could go back in time, I wouldn't do things any other way.

Love,

Adora

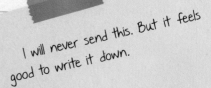

I will never send this. But it feels good to write it down.

THE END?

So much has happened since I began this report.
I know a lot more about being She-Ra than I did
when I started. I learned a lot of other things, too.

I learned that:

- WHEN MY FRIENDS
  AND I STICK TOGETHER,
  WE CAN DO ANYTHING.

- SOME THINGS ARE
  WORTH FIGHTING FOR.

- SOMETIMES, ENEMIES CAN
  BECOME ALLIES.

- I AM STRONG ENOUGH TO BE
  SHE-RA—STRONGER THAN I
  THOUGHT.

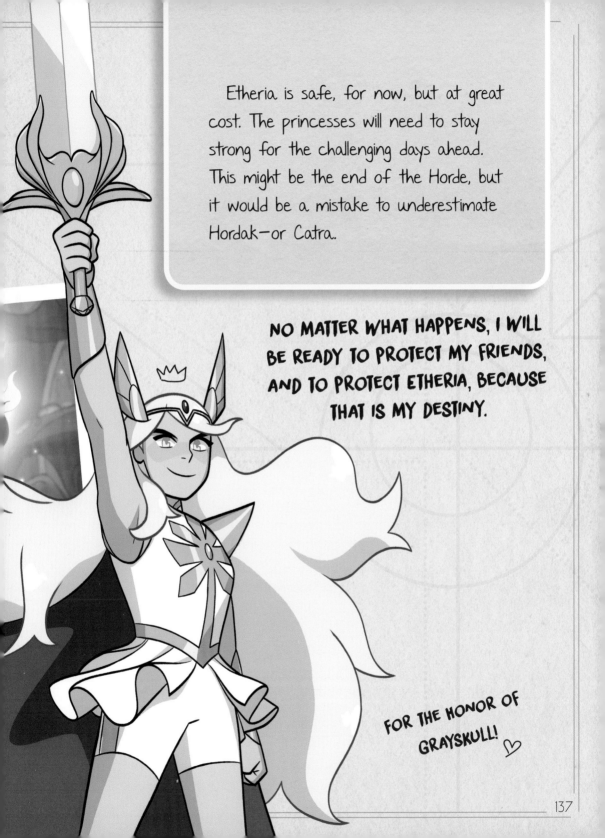

Etheria is safe, for now, but at great cost. The princesses will need to stay strong for the challenging days ahead. This might be the end of the Horde, but it would be a mistake to underestimate Hordak—or Catra.

NO MATTER WHAT HAPPENS, I WILL BE READY TO PROTECT MY FRIENDS, AND TO PROTECT ETHERIA, BECAUSE THAT IS MY DESTINY.

FOR THE HONOR OF GRAYSKULL!